The Adventures of Princess Pauline, Prince Ademola Jnr and their Blue Dragon

Ademola Usuanlele

DEDICATION

To:

Dr Warren & Mrs. Lois Hathaway *(My Canadian Parents)*

Mr. Richard & Mrs. Hannah Usuanlele *(Parents, RIP)*

Prince Olu Eweka *(Brother, RIP)*

Mrs. Adunni Enogieru Momoh *(Sister, RIP)*

Mr. Nosa Usuanlele *(Brother, RIP)*

Mr. Isaac Omolayo Kolade *(Cousin, RIP)*

APPRECIATION

To God be all the Glory! I want to use this opportunity to thank God and to thank all of you for your support during the writing of these books. I give special thanks to my bosses; Christiana, Pauline and Ademola Jnr for their feedback and supervision and because of whom these books were written. Adebisi

Usuanlele, Joyce Usuanlele, Sue Robins, Emmy Otoijamun, Rtd General Adamu & Mrs Doreen Yusuf, Dr. Jean Walrond and Susan Abraham thanks for your support, reviews and editing of these books. Thanks to Bishop Emmanuel & Mrs. Bridget Jatau, Pastor Joseph & Pastor (Mrs) Joanna Odidi, Pastor Daniel & Mrs. Grace Adewumi, Late Mr. Isaac and Mrs. Monisola Kolade and Pastor Clement Igbinidu and members of Winners Chapel International Edmonton for your prayers, spiritual and wise Godly counsel. Nick Imoru, Pastor Olayioye Abraham and Dale Youngman thanks a million times for your publishing support. Merci beaucoup!

Part A

THE STORY OF PRINCESS PAULINE, MR. KONGI & THE BLUE DRAGON

Once upon a time in the Kingdom of Edmonton, there lived a very pretty and beautiful Princess calledPauline. She has a little brother called "Mr. Kongi". His real name is Ademola Jnr. or Joseph. Mr. Kongi is a good kid but often misunderstood

In the Kingdom of Edmonton, there were many different dragons with different colours. Of all the dragons, the friendliest and prettiest was the Blue and Yellow Dragon. This Blue Dragon was a good friend of Princess Pauline and her brother Mr. Kongi.

There came a time in the Kingdom of Edmonton that war was approaching, and trouble-makers were coming very close to the kingdom. The King and Queen decided that it would be best to take Princess Pauline and her brother Mr. Kongi to another kingdom where they will be okay and safe.

The Blue Dragon volunteered to take her friends Princess Pauline and Mr. Kongi to this kingdom. They agreed that it will be safer to undertake this journey at night.

Finally the night of the journey came. The Blue Dragon got ready and flew to the Palace where Princess Pauline and Mr. Kongi were staying to pick them up.

Princess Pauline wore her best princess dress and Mr. Kongi put on his best robe. They hugged and kissed their parents, the King and Queen, goodbye. The Queen was crying when she told the Blue Dragon "Please take good care of my little sweethearts."

Then, Princess Pauline and Mr. Kongi jumped on the back of their friend the Blue Dragon. So the journey began. It was very dark, so dark that The Blue Dragon could not see past her nose.

Since it was very dark, the Blue Dragon decided to use her special gift that was a breath of fire. The Blue Dragon breathed fi re, and it gave off a light as she flew. She did this until they got to the Kingdom of London. It was a very long journey. They travelled through the night and got to the Kingdom of London in the early hours of the next morning.

Part B

THE PARTY FOR PRINCESS PAULINE,
MR. KONGI & THE BLUE DRAGON
IN THE KINGDOM OF LONDON

When Princess Pauline, Mr. Kongi and the Blue Dragon got to the Kingdom of London, they got a big surprise! All the other Princesses and Princes from all the other Kingdoms, including the Kingdom of London, were waiting for them to arrive.

The Princesses and the Princes of all the Kingdoms were going to have a special party to welcome Princess Pauline, Mr. Kongi and the Blue Dragon to the Kingdom of London.

At the party, there was all the good stuff for young Princesses and Princes to relax and enjoy themselves. Good stuff like fun games, rides, and to cap it all off, there were great foods like salads, meatloaf, hot dogs, hamburgers, chicken, beef, goat meat, cakes of all kinds, all kinds of ice-cream, and finally, there were fruits of all kinds and chocolates of all kinds. The young Princesses and Princes had all kinds of juices and chocolate milk.

The young Princesses and Princes celebrated this great party for three days. They had so much to eat and drink. They were all full and satisfi ed. They said a very big thank you to the King and Queen of the Kingdom of London for paying for such a fancy party for Princess Pauline, Mr. Kongi, the Blue Dragon and all the other Princesses and Princes from the other Kingdoms.

Then it was time to sleep in the Kingdom of London. So all the young Princesses and Princes brushed their teeth, took a bath, put on their pajamas, and read their bedtime stories before going to sleep.

Princess Pauline, Mr. Kongi and the Blue Dragon recalled all the activities for the last few days and went to sleep with a smile on their faces.

Part C

THE JOURNEY TO THE NORTH POLE BY PRINCESS PAULINE, MR. KONGI & THE BLUE DRAGON TO HELP SANTA CLAUS SAVE CHRISTMAS

Princess Pauline's and Mr. Kongi's birthday parties had just ended, and there was only ten days before Christmas. The snow was already on the ground and there were gentle flakes of snow falling on the ground in the Kingdom of Edmonton. Suddenly, the phone rang, and it was from Santa Claus in the North Pole.

Princess Pauline, Mr. Kongi and the Blue Dragon got very excited, and they all rushed to answer the phone to talk to Santa Claus. Santa told them there was a very big problem. They asked Santa, "What was the very big problem?"

Santa answered, "There will be no gifts for all the children of the world this Christmas."

Princess Pauline, Mr. Kongi and the Blue Dragon screamed, "What!! Santa, why?"

Princess Pauline, Mr. Kongi and the Blue Dragon asked, "Santa, why won't the Children get their presents this Christmas?"

"I have a big situation in the North Pole," said Santa.

"All the reindeers and all the Elves and Santa's helpers are now too old to fi nish making the gifts and to help Santa give out all the gifts on Christmas Eve."

Santa asked Princess Pauline, Mr. Kongi and the Blue Dragon if they could help.
They joyfully said, "Yes!" but asked Santa to ask their parents if it was ok. Santa asked their parents or permission to have them come to the North Pole to help with making and giving out the gifts

The parents of Princess Pauline, Mr. Kongi and the Blue Dragon said yes!

The next day, Princess Pauline, Mr. Kongi and the Blue Dragon got ready and began their journey to the North Pole.

They got a GPS and asked NORAD to help guide them to Santa's house in the North Pole. It was a very long journey. They flew past vast expanse of land and then snow and ice before they got to the North Pole. The journey was made easier by their GPS and the help from NORAD.

When they got to Santa's house in the North Pole, they were surprised to see how pretty and big the house was. Santa Claus came running to give them a very big hug and welcome them to the North Pole. They were excited, and the Elves, Santa helpers, Mrs. Claus and the reindeers were all very, very happy and excited to see Princess Pauline, Mr. Kongi and the Blue Dragon. They were all very excited that Princess Pauline, Mr. Kongi and the Blue Dragon were going to help them save Christmas and the Children of the world will get their presents on Christmas Eve.

Mrs. Claus was especially very excited to meet them. She made special dishes and yummy desserts and treats for them to eat. She said:

"Go to bed early because tomorrow work starts for the gifts wrapping before the journey around the world to distribute the gifts to all the Children of the world on Christmas Eve."

The work days were very long, and the work was sometimes hard, but it was fun work. Mrs. Claus

provided a lot of treats for everyone in Santa's house.

On December 22, everything was ready except for one big problem. Santa Claus found Mr. Kongi's name on the not-so-good list. It means that Mr. Kongi will only get a little present for Christmas. There was a big grumbling in Santa's house. Everyone asked that Mr. Kongi's name be moved from the not-sogood list to the Good Kid list, because of all his efforts in the North Pole to save Christmas for Children of the world. Santa Claus agreed, and there was a big cheer, and Mr. Kongi was very happy and excited and he promised to be a good kid all the time and every time.

On December 23rd, there was a small party in the North Pole to celebrate the completion of preparation. Mrs. Claus made sure there was a lot of food to eat and drinks to drink. After the food and drinks, it was time to go to bed early before the big day. So everyone went to bed, and the North Pole was quiet.

The morning of December 24, i.e., Christmas Eve - the day before the big day - Christmas Day.

The Blue Dragon stepped out for all the Christmas gifts of all the Children of the world to be loaded on her before the journey around the world began. Mr. Kongi and Princess Pauline were going to go with Santa on this journey. They all quickly ate their lunches and hopped on the Blue Dragon, and so began the journey around the world.

With the help of NORAD and GPS, the Blue Dragon took Santa Claus, Princess Pauline and Mr. Kongi to all the houses around the world to deliver a surprise Christmas gift for the Children.

They completed their mission and were back to the North Pole just before midnight on Christmas Eve. Everyone was excited to have them back to the North Pole, and it was a very fun experience for everyone and they were all relieved they made it back safely.

At Midnight, they shouted Merry Christmas to one another, quickly opened their presents from Santa and Mrs. Claus. They were pretty and fun toys and games. It was getting too late in the night, so Mrs. Claus asked everyone to go to bed to get some sleep to be up in time for breakfast.

At breakfast time, Santa and Mrs. Claus broke the news that Princess Pauline, Mr. Kongi and the Blue Dragon will be returning to the kingdom of Edmonton. To join their parents for Christmas lunch and

open more Christmas presents when they get there.

Mrs. Claus asked Princess Pauline, Mr. Kongi and The Blue Dragon to come back on December 16th, the day after the Kongi's Birthday, to help Santa Claus for the next five years. There was another big cheer from everyone in Santa's house.

Then it was time for Princess Pauline, Mr. Kongi and the Blue Dragon to leave the North Pole. There were cheers, tears, and clapping. Santa Claus brought some more presents for them.

He told Mr. Kongi, "You are a good kid, and one day you will be Santa Claus."

Mr. Kongi smiled and said, "Thank you Santa and Mrs. Claus."

Princess Pauline and Mr. Kongi jumped on the Blue Dragon's back and began the long journey home to the Kingdom of Edmonton.

As promised, Princess Pauline, Mr. Kongi, and The Blue Dragon returned every December 16th for the next five years to the North Pole. They returned to the North Pole to help Santa and Mrs. Claus and all the elves; reindeers and helpers make, wrap and distribute Christmas presents.

Part D

PRINCE ADEMOLA JNR BECOMES SANTA CLAUS AND PRINCESS PAULINE BECOMES CHIEF SANTA HELPER

Exactly five years since Princess Pauline and her brother Mr. Kongi last went to the North Pole. They went to help Santa Claus to prepare, package and distribute gifts to all the children of the world on Christmas Eve. It was summer in the North Pole and the Kingdom of Edmonton. All the leaves and grass were all vibrant, and there were very beautiful and lovely flowers everywhere. It was a sweet-smelling aroma in the air.

It was about 5pm in the evening. The phone rang and guess who was on the phone? It was Mr. and Mrs. Santa Claus. Princess Pauline and Mr. Kongi got very excited, and they were jumping for joy. They completely forgot that Mr. and Mrs. Santa Claus were waiting to talk to them on the phone. Princess Pauline and Mr. Kongi finally remembered that Mr. and Mrs. Claus were on the phone waiting.

When Princess Pauline and Mr. Kongi got to the phone, they apologized for the long hold time because they just were filled with excitement. Mr. Santa Claus asked Princess Pauline and Mr. Kongi how they were doing with school work and helping to keep the Palace tidy and clean. Princess Pauline replied "school is great and fun, and our grades are getting better by the term". For the Palace tidiness, they are doing their best to help but the workers in the Palace are not letting her and her brother do much.

Princess Pauline and Mr. Kongi thanked Mr. and Mrs. Santa Claus for all the opportunities they got in Santa's house in the North Pole to learn a lot of life skills and house-keeping skills. Santa Claus asked Princess Pauline and Mr. Kongi if the King and Queen are in residence? Princess Pauline said yes! He asked Princess Pauline to find out if they can speak to the King and Queen on the phone. Princess Pauline told them to hold on for a minute so that they can go find out from the King and Queen.

Princess Pauline and Mr. Kongi ran to the King and Queen's chambers. They said: "Daddy! Daddy!! Mr. and Mrs. Santa Claus are on the phone. They would like to speak to you." The King said, "please transfer the call over. Thank you, guys,!" Princess Pauline and Mr. Kongi went back to Mr. and Mrs. Claus on the phone. They informed

Santa and Mrs. Claus that the king would like to talk to them. The line was quickly transferred to the King and Queen.

"Hello Santa and Mrs. Claus!" said the King. Santa replied: "Your Highness! Ho Ho Ho. After the exchange of greetings between the King and Queen and Mr. Santa and Mrs. Claus, they settled down for a real chat. Santa Claus informed the King that they were on a summer holiday in the Kingdom of Calgary which is quite close to the Kingdom of Edmonton. They would like an audience with the King and Queen in the Kingdom of Edmonton to discuss some proposed changes in the North Pole. They checked all their calendars and they agreed that they would "meet on Thursday; three days from today for an all you can eat buffet from 12:00 noon until 1pm in the Palace in the Kingdom of Edmonton. The meeting will start at 1:15pm".

It was a Thursday and a beautiful summer day. All the birds were singing in the trees; there were many butterflies on the flowers and the leaves on the trees were as green as they can be. The much-anticipated guests arrived at the Palace of the Kingdom of Edmonton. Mr. and Mrs. Claus arrived at 11:45am. They were warmly welcomed and escorted to the dining hall of the Palace. Princess Pauline and her brother; Mr. Kongi were seated eagerly waiting for Mr. and Mrs. Claus to arrive. They were very happy and excited to see Mr. and Mrs. Santa Claus again. They could not leave their seats because the King told them that no running around and talking while eating in the dining hall and dining table. So, they obeyed the rule.

The King and the Queen stepped out of their chambers and looked elegant and radiant. They walked down majestically to the

table everyone stood up until they were both seated. They sat on their usual King and Queen chairs. The delicious meal was ready to be eaten. The special item on the menu today was Alberta Beef raised in the Kingdom of Edmonton. Princess Pauline was asked to bless the food. She blessed the food promptly. Then everyone started eating in silence for 45 minutes.

After the sumptuous meal, everyone decided to take a break to allow the food to digest. At about 1:15pm Mr. and Mrs. Claus were both invited to have an audience with the King and Queen of Edmonton Kingdom. They both bowed their heads for the King and Queen as they entered the King's Court. They were directed to their seats. The King and Queen asked Mr Santa Claus and Mrs. Claus what brought them to seek the audience of His Royal Highness. The

King told them "you may speak". Santa Claus asked the King "where do I start from your majesty?" "Anywhere!" Said the King.

Mr. Santa Claus told the King that Mrs. Claus and he were retiring from being Santa Claus and Mrs. Claus in the North Pole. They would like to travel around the world now while their knees, ankles and waist can still take such a beating. He said they had travelled around the world many a Christmas Eve, and they have chosen Princess Pauline and her brother Mr. Kongi (Prince Ademola Jnr) to become Mr. Santa Claus and the Chief Santa Helper. The statement made Princess Pauline and Mr. Kongi scream out: "Whaaaaaat!" Out of sheer excitement and joy even though they were saddened about Mr. Santa Claus and Mrs. Claus retiring. The Queen turned to them and said: "Shhh!"

Santa Claus told the King and Queen that they were confident that Princess Pauline and Prince Ademola Jnr can run the operations in the North Pole without a hitch. The reason is that they have the hands-on experience; having gone through all the basic training during their numerous trips to help in the North Pole. They know everyone there, and they get along with everyone in Santa's house. The King asked Princess Pauline and Prince Ademola Jnr if they would like to take up the assignment in the North Pole as Santa Claus and Chief Santa Helper. They screamed "Yes! Yes!! Yes!!!"

The King and Queen were delighted that Princess Pauline and Mr. Kongi are interested in the new assignment. The King and Queen stepped up from the throne to bless Princess Pauline and Prince Ademola Jnr for the mission they will be embarking on in the name

of his Majesty the King of Edmonton. The King mentioned that they must return every summer to play with him the King and their mother, the Queen. Santa Claus and Mrs. Claus were very happy and grateful for the King's approval and the decision of Princess Pauline and Mr. Kongi to take over the role of Santa Claus and the Chief Santa Helper.

The King ordered that the preparations are to start immediately. Their schooling is going to be online and distance learning. The Blue Dragon will go with them, and video-conferencing facilities must be set up for them to chat with the King and Queen while they are in the North Pole. Mr. Kongi raised his hand to be permitted to speak, and the King gave him the permission to speak. He said he is worried because he does not have white hair and white

beards to be like Santa Claus. Santa Claus told him that they would make special "pretend" hair and beards for him in the North Pole. The King announced that the departure date for Princess Pauline and Prince Ademola Jnr to the North Pole would be August 15.

After several weeks of preparations and planning, the departure date arrived. It was a bright sunny summer day on August 15 in the Kingdom of Edmonton. The Blue Dragon arrived as early as 5am from the Galaxyland where she lives. She said she arrived so early because she was too excited to sleep for much longer. The departure time was scheduled for 9am after breakfast which was scheduled for 7:30am to 8:30am. To meet up to this schedule, they decided to start loading all the stuff Princess Pauline and Prince Ademola Jnr were taking to the North Pole. All the baggage was

loaded on the back of the Blue Dragon. Then it was time to go have breakfast with the Queen and King.

Princess Pauline and Prince Ademola Jnr were at the dining hall and were seated at the royal dining table waiting patiently for their Mummy (Queen) and Daddy (King) to arrive at the dining table. The King and Queen of the Kingdom of Edmonton arrived at the Royal Dining table at 7:30am. The King asked Mr. Kongi to bless the food which he did. After which they all settled down and ate their breakfast in silence according to the Palace rule of no talking while eating. Mr. Kongi and Princess Pauline observed that the Queen was in tears throughout the breakfast time, but they could not ask any question about it because of the silence during meal time in the Palace.

Immediately after breakfast, Princess Pauline and her brother Mr. Kongi ran around the dining table to meet their mum the Queen to find out why she was crying. She told them that she was crying because of the mixed feelings about their trip to the North Pole. She said she was happy because they were going to learn valuable skills and knowledge that will someday make them become a great King and a great Queen. The Queen also said that she is sad to let her precious son and daughter go live so far away and that she and the King will miss them so much.

The King joined the conversation by telling the Queen that Princess Pauline and Mr. Kongi will have video-conferencing, satellite phones, GPS and support from NORAD. The King mentioned that Princess Pauline and Prince Ademola Jnr planned to visit every

summer; that is their off season in the North Pole. Also, they plan to have a quick stop over for tea with you and me on Christmas Eve during their annual journey to distribute gifts to the children of the world including children of the Palace staff. With these assurances from the King, the Queen stopped crying and put on her majestic face, and she was ready to see the Princess and Prince depart to the North Pole.

Now it was time to go from the Kingdom of Edmonton to the North Pole. The Blue Dragon was all set for the trip, and he had all the materials Princess Pauline and Prince Ademola Jnr needed for their stay in the North Pole. The King and Queen gave Princess Pauline and Prince Ademola Jnr lots of hugs and kisses and all the Palace staff gave them three rounds of applause.

The Blue Dragon lowered himself for Princess Pauline and Prince Ademola Jnr to climb into the basket where they will seat throughout the journey. The Queen packed three sets of lunch for the Blue Dragon, Princess Pauline and Prince Ademola Jnr to eat at lunch time on their way to the North Pole. Princess Pauline and Prince Ademola Jnr simultaneously blew kisses to everyone including the King and Queen. Then the long journey began.

All their previous trips to the North Pole have been in the winter season. It was their first trip in the summer season to the North Pole. They saw all kinds of vegetation and few animals running around in the Tundra including polar bears and their little cubs. A lot of the snow and ice were melted, and they saw the bare ground in some places because of the summer temperatures. They decided it was a

great time to eat their lunches. They took a 30-minute break to eat. After the lunch break, they were on the move again towards the North Pole, which was two and one-half hours away. They flew non-stop to get to the North Pole in time for the Grande reception that awaited them in the North Pole.

They arrived at the North Pole at 5:15pm on August 15. They were immediately ushered into the giant Igloo at the North Pole where Mr. Santa Claus and Mrs. Claus and Santa's household lived. Everybody was very excited about Princess Pauline and Prince Ademola Jnr and the Blue Dragon. There was a welcome party for them at 6pm. So, they decided to quickly setup the video-conferencing system to call their mummy and daddy; the King and Queen of the Kingdom of Edmonton.

They made the calls, and there was a big relief for the King and Queen that they arrived safely to the North Pole. It was a brief call because Princess Pauline and Prince Ademola Jnr needed to clean up and dress up for the party in their honour. At exactly 6pm in the North Pole everyone was ready and waiting for the special guests; the Princess, the Prince and their special friend the Blue Dragon. When they walked into the reception hall, there was a big round of applause for them.

Santa quickly rang the bell to bring the attention to him. He said: "You all know why we are here. It is a welcome party for Princess Pauline, Prince Ademola Jnr and the Blue Dragon to the North Pole. They are becoming the new Santa Claus and the Chief Santa Helper". There was another round of applause for them. With that, Santa

Claus declared the party open. He said: "Enjoy yourselves". There were all kinds of food and drinks and desserts, and there were fun games. And the goodies were made available for the party. Princess Pauline gave the vote of thanks. She said: "We are very happy and grateful for this honourable party put together by everyone. We truly feel welcomed and appreciated and we promised Mr. Santa Claus and Mrs. Claus that we will not let them down in this our new roles.

About 30 minutes after the party ended, Prince Ademola was asked to come kit up in his full Santa Claus regalia. After 15 minutes in the room, he stepped out with full Santa Claus regalia including the "pretend hair and beards". He went straight to Santa Claus' chair and sat down on it. Santa Claus asked "Prince Ademola Jnr how is the

Santa Claus suit?" His reply was: "Ho Ho Ho Ho Ho". Then Santa asked him: "How is the pretend beard and hair?" He replied: "Ho Ho Ho Ho Ho". Santa asked him: "How was the welcome party and the accompanying dinner?" The new young Santa replied: "Ho Ho Ho Ho Ho". To that everybody stood up and gave him five rounds of applause and he got handshakes and hugs from everyone in the room. The old Santa Claus was overwhelmed with mixed emotions that he was shedding tears and laughing at the same time. He said: "Thank you God. We have a new Santa in the house."

Part E

THE YOUNG SANTA CLAUS AND HIS CHIEF SANTA HELPER

The day after the welcome party, Prince Ademola Jnr commenced his role as Santa Claus and his sister Princess Pauline became the Chief Santa Helper. The day was August 16, and there were two weeks before the preparation for this year's gifts for the children of the world on Christmas Eve. Santa asked everyone in the North Pole to take any holidays that they have not taken before September 1 when the preparation was starting. Everyone was excited to take holidays before the work started.

Then came September 1 the Kick-off date. Everyone came in for a quick preparation kick off meeting. In his first address to the entire North Pole team, the young Santa encouraged everyone to do their assigned tasks very well and safely. He asked that they should all take their breaks and resume work and close from work as scheduled. He also asked that if anyone is not sure or comfortable with any tasks they should feel free to ask for another task. He wished the entire team God Speed!

The work started in earnest; the list for the children were all logged into a computer system. The computer system generated the names and types of toys on each child's list, and production was done daily based on the request on the system, and packaging and labeling were done based on the log. The Santa's team produced

the toys using Just In Time (JIT) production. Which means only logged items are produced to save time and avoid wastage of materials or producing items that are not assigned to a child

This process continued until all the gifts for all the world's children were produced, packaged and labeled. For this first year for the young Santa, the project was completed on the 20th of December. Thereby giving Santa three days before the delivery date of December 24. The Chief Santa Helper was exhausted, and she needed the three days before the journey date. She had spent most of her time supervising and coaching the various production teams. Santa gave everyone on the North Pole three days off before the D-Day – 24th of December.

Today is the D-Day i.e. Delivery Day of the gifts to all the children of the world, and the date is December 24. Everyone woke up a little early to help load up all the gifts on the Blue Dragon and Santa's Reindeers. Within three hours, all the items were loaded up. Princess Pauline, the Chief Santa Helper, hopped on the Blue Dragon and Mr. Kongi the new young Santa hopped on the Blue Dragon. They both blew kisses to every one of the Santa's house in the North Pole. After which Santa and his Chief Helper checked all their gears like GPS, Satellite Phones, NORAD system and the regular phone. All systems were okay. They packed some snacks like chicken nuggets and fruits and juices to snack on the way.

"Okay let us go!" said Santa to the Chief Santa Helper and the Blue Dragon and the Reindeers and off they went. Their first

destination was the Kingdom of Australia and New Zealand and all other kingdoms along the way as they moved westward. They used the log and GPS and the support of NORAD to guide their way to the various houses in all the countries on the list. They needed to be quick because there were a lot of places to visit.

As the night progressed, they were on track going from one kingdom to another dropping off presents for the children of the world under their Christmas trees while the children were sleeping. The hope is that they would find the presents under their Christmas trees when they wake up on Christmas day morning. When they arrived at the Kingdom of London, they were going from house to house based on the names and addresses on the log they were using. Finally, there was only one house left in the Kingdom of London in the Borough of Chelsea.

This house left in the Borough of Chelsea in the Kingdom of London somehow created a problem for Santa Claus. The reason is that there was a little boy called Ted Johnson who was awake and seated by the Christmas tree. He was eating Santa's milk and cookies and waiting for Santa Claus to show up so that he can make his case why he should be put on the good list instead of the not-so-good list. After waiting for Ted Johnson to fall asleep for half an hour, Santa decided to go into the house through the furnace to meet with Ted and find out why he was waiting to chat with Santa Claus.

When Santa got into the house, he immediately carried Ted and placed him on his lap and asked him: "What is your name young man?" Ted replied: "Ted Johnson." Santa responded: "Ho Ho Ho Ho Ho". Santa asked him: "Why are you not sleeping like everyone else in

your family?" Ted told Santa that he was waiting to see Santa to explain his situation that led to his name being put on the not-so-good list. Ted said whenever his Daddy was not home his three senior sisters usually gang up on him to oppress him and to bully him. He had to stand his ground and protect himself. Santa said he would remove Ted's name from the not-so-good list and move it to the good list.

Santa told Ted in return for moving his name to the good list, Ted should stop fighting with his sisters, and he should be nice to them all the time. Santa promised Ted that he would talk to his mom and dad so that they can diffuse the tension in the house. Santa gave Ted two presents instead of one. He also left two presents for each of Ted's three sisters. Ted thanked Santa for his love and

understanding, and Santa gave Ted a big hug and left Ted's house.

When Santa came out of Ted's house to join his Chief Helper; Princess Pauline and the Blue Dragon, they were almost sleeping off due to boredom. Princess Pauline asked Santa why it took so long to come out of Ted's house. She said: "We are running behind for the time and remember that we promised our daddy and mummy that we will be visiting to have a quick tea with them".

Santa explained to Princess Pauline and the Blue Dragon the reason he spent some time with Ted and the follow up plan of contacting Ted's parents in January to diffuse the tension between Ted and his three senior sisters. Santa Claus asked his Chief Helper to record the follow-up call in the log for January 3 next year. Now it

was time to leave the Kingdom of London and cross the mighty Atlantic Ocean to get to the Kingdoms of the Americas. After several hours of flying the Blue Dragon got to the first Kingdom in the Americas; the Kingdom of New Foundland and Labrador.

From the Kingdom of New Foundland and Labrador, they visited the home of all other children in the other Kingdoms in Canada and the United States of America, Central America including the Caribbean and South America. They also made one very important stop in the Kingdom of Edmonton to have a quick 15-minute tea break with their daddy and mummy; the King and Queen of the Kingdom of Edmonton. Santa Claus and his Chief Helper were very happy to see the King and Queen. They chatted over tea and cookies. They left all the gifts they brought for all the

children in the Palace ground with the King and Queen so that they can share them along with their gifts for the children.

They departed the Kingdom of Edmonton to their final stop that was the Kingdom of Hawaii from which they departed after sharing the Christmas gifts to the children in the Kingdom of Hawaii. They returned to the North Pole at 11:45pm on December 24. There was a huge jubilation in Santa's house. Everyone was happy to see Santa, his Chief Helper, and the Blue Dragon return safely and sound from their Christmas gifts sharing mission all by themselves. Suddenly, Santa rang the big bell and shouted: "Merry Christmas! Ho Ho Ho Ho and everyone in Santa's house shouted Merry Christmas! There were hugs and kisses and handshakes. Then it was time for everyone to open their presents. There were lots of shouting and jumping for joy

because everyone got all they asked for from Santa. They were all very grateful to Santa and his Chief Helper.

Santa and his Chief Helper thanked everyone and told them that without their hard work and efforts the mission would have been impossible. The room that contains all the Christmas treats was opened by Princess Pauline, the Santa's Chief Helper. She informed everyone to enjoy themselves with the treats, but they should remember to enjoy themselves responsibly. At 2:30am on Christmas day the party ended and everyone in Santa's house went to bed. At 9am on Christmas day, the bell for breakfast was rung in the North Pole. Everybody came out for breakfast yawning because of little sleep. The breakfast was quick after which some went back to bed, and others decided to go for more treats from the "treats" room.

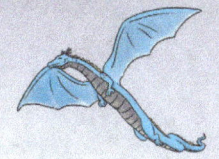

The merriment continued right up to New Year's Day at Santa's house by members of Santa's household. On the 2nd of January, Santa called for a review meeting to look at all the activities of the last gift-giving season. So that they can understand what worked well and what did not work well so that they can be improved. After the review by all key task managers and stakeholders along with Santa and the Chief Santa Helper, some few improvements were recommended. They were assigned to the affected task managers to perform them and report back to the review committee at the end of February.

January 3 was finally here, the day Santa Claus promised to call Ted Johnson's parents after the encounter with Ted in the Kingdom of

London on the 24th of December. It was during the gift-giving mission around the world for the children all over the world. Santa and the Chief Santa Helper called Ted's parents at 8pm local time in the Kingdom of London. His parents were excited to talk to Santa Claus and his Chief Helper. Santa and Chief Helper explained to Ted's parents about Santa's encounter with Ted on December 24. They asked Ted's parents to find ways to reduce the conflicts between Ted and his three older sisters and to try to increase their cooperation and friendliness. Santa said he believes that Ted is a good kid, and he sees the potential for a very great kid. That is why he doubled his presents last Christmas.

Mr. and Mrs. Johnson; Ted's parents were happy about this chat with Santa and his Chief Helper. They promised that they will do their best

to ensure that Ted becomes a very great kid with all these potentials he has. The call ended there, and Santa Claus and his Chief Helper decided to study their books and catch up on their homework that was piling up since the Christmas and New Year holidays. They took a break after a few hours of studying to have a video-conferencing with their mama and papa; the King and Queen of the Kingdom of Edmonton. The King and Queen were very happy as usual to see the pretty faces of Princess Pauline and Prince Ademola Jnr. The King and Queen wanted to know how things were going in Santa's house in the North Pole. Princess Pauline answered: "Ho Ho Ho Ho Ho." And she said: "Sometimes chaotic but we are usually able to bring things back under control". The King asked them about their studies, and they said everything was going fine.

After 10 minutes of chatting with the King and Queen, it was time to return to studies. They blew kisses to the King and Queen and then ended the call. They studied for another two hours before taking a break for the day to relax and play some games before dinner. During the dinner, Santa Claus announced to everybody in Santa's house that this year's break will commence on February 15 and end on September 15. So that everyone can have more time to themselves should they want to travel or continue their online studies like him and his Chief Helper. The holiday will be a paid holiday for everyone said Santa's Chief Helper. Everyone cheered and applauded the announcements, and they were all joyful. They sang "he is a jolly good fellow" for two minutes until Santa asked them to finish their dinner especially when they were supposed to be quiet when eating.

Time flew by so fast that it was February 15 the day after Valentine's Day. Everyone in Santa's house in the North Pole was all set for their holidays/breaks. The plan was the same across the board three months for studies online and three months for traveling and holidays across the world. Santa Claus and his Chief Helper and the Blue Dragon will study online until May 14 and then travel to the Kingdom of Edmonton on May 15. As promised to spend the summer with the King and Queen and everyone in the King's Palace. The North Pole was very calm and quiet for the next three months. As a result of more than 50% of the people in Santa's household chose to travel for their first three months to escape the last half of the winter season in the North Pole. Princess Pauline and her brother Prince Ademola Jnr were able to concentrate on their online studies. They

covered a lot of materials, and they got excellent grades in all their assessments. The King and Queen of Edmonton were very pleased with their results.

By May 14, Princess Pauline and Prince Ademola Jnr were able to cover a full school year's materials in the three months of their intensive online studies. In the night of May 14, Princess Pauline, Prince Ademola Jnr; the Santa Claus and his Chief Helper and the Blue Dragon packed their entire luggage. In preparation for their trip on May 15 to the Kingdom of Edmonton. Their plan was to leave just after breakfast at 8am. Their sleep was sweet but short because of the excitement of traveling the next day. After breakfast, they set out for their trip to the Kingdom of Edmonton. The journey was fast. They arrived at the Kingdom of Edmonton at 12noon on May 15 in time for

lunch with the King and Queen in the Palace. The King and Queen were very happy to see them. They gave Princess Pauline and Prince Ademola Jnr lots of hugs and kisses. They decided to proceed to the dining chamber of the Palace to eat lunch.

At the dining table, to Princess Pauline's and Prince Ademola's surprise the menu on the table included Japanese cuisine, Italian cuisine in addition to the usual North American cuisine. Princess Pauline likes Japanese cuisine especially the sushi and Prince Ademola Jnr likes Italian cuisine especially pepperoni pizza. They all quickly settled down to eat the sumptuous lunch after which they all went to the King's court within the Palace to chat. Princess Pauline (Chief Santa Helper) and Prince Ademola Jnr (Santa Claus) thanked the King and Queen for the great lunch. They proceeded to brief the

King and Queen about their mission to the North Pole and their work so far as Santa Claus and Chief Santa Helper. They also discussed their school work. The Queen and King were very impressed about their progress in all areas. The King was especially impressed at the way they are running the operations at the North Pole and in Santa's house. For that statement, Prince Ademola Jnr responded: "Ho Ho Ho Ho Ho".

For the next three months, the King, Queen, Princess and Prince enjoyed their time together doing various fun stuff like hiking, fishing, watching movies, playing board games and video games. The King and Queen gave them training in the areas of roles and responsibilities of being a King and a Queen. Princess Pauline and Prince Ademola Jnr enjoyed the training. They loved the fun part of

being a King and Queen. However, they were sort of surprised at the responsibilities that come with being a King and a Queen. Their parents assured them that once they get crowned, the Spirit of God becomes their guide and protector and inspiration. This statement calmed their nerves. Before they knew it, September 14 arrived, and it was time to return to the North Pole to be Santa Claus and Chief Santa Helper again. They bade good-byes and got hugs and kisses from the King and Queen, and they departed for the North Pole after breakfast and they arrived at North Pole during lunch hour. They joined the crew for lunch in the North Pole. Most of the team members arrived at the North Pole on September 14 in preparation for work. Work for the next Christmas began on September 15.

"After the long break, it was really good to see everyone refreshed and energized for the preparation for the next Christmas

project," said Santa Claus. "I cannot agree more" said Princess Pauline; Santa's Chief Helper. The next morning the bells for breakfast sounded at 7am. Everyone came in for breakfast in time for work to resume at 8am and end at 5pm with a one-hour lunch break at 12noon including two 15-minute breaks in-between from Mondays to Fridays. Saturdays and Sundays were the time off for everyone. This schedule of work was maintained until the work was finished, and everything for Santa and his Chief Helper gifts-giving on December 24 was ready. With the process improvement implemented, it took the team less time to prepare. They were through with gifts making by December 18. Santa gave them five days off for a job well done and a very loud Ho Ho Ho Ho.

After the five days off in the North Pole, it was time to load up all the gifts for all the children of the world to open and celebrate with

them on Christmas day. The gifts were a lot more than the previous year's gifts. The Blue Dragon said she was okay with the loaded gifts for the trip. It was time for Santa Claus, The Chief Santa Helper and the Blue Dragon to take off. They got hugs and kisses from the crew and took off for the journey. The journey around the world was going smoothly from one Kingdom to another Kingdom until they got to their last stop in the Borough of Chelsea in the Kingdom of London. They double-checked their records, and it turned out to be Ted Johnson's house. The light was on again, and Santa saw him sitting patiently by the Christmas tree with a large jug of milk and lots of deliciously looking large cookies and biscuits.

Santa Claus and his Chief Helper entered Ted's house using the secret entrance. Ted was shocked, and he quickly recovered due to

the excitement and he got up and gave Santa Claus and his Chief Helper a big hug. Santa wanted to find out why he was awake at this time of the night. Ted said he wanted to have a chat and eat the cookies, biscuits and drink the milk with Santa. Ted ran to the kitchen to grab a third glass for Santa's Chief Helper to join them in the refreshments. Santa Claus asked Ted how things were going with him and his three sisters and with his parents. He said: "everything is sweet now; no fights, no yelling and it is one big happy family thanks to you Santa". They chatted about a few other items and then it was time to continue the mission of gift-giving to the remaining kids around the world that night. Before Santa Claus and the Chief Helper left they dropped off three gifts for Ted and two each for his three sisters. They gave Ted hugs and left the Kingdom of London.

Santa Claus, the Chief Helper, and the Blue Dragon left Ted's house

in the Kingdom of London to head to the Kingdoms in the Americas and Island of Hawaii. They were able to complete all their assignment including a brief stop as promised in the Kingdom of Edmonton to have tea with their mummy and daddy – the Queen and King of the Kingdom of Edmonton. The King and Queen were very happy to see Santa and the Chief Helper and the Blue Dragon. From Edmonton, Santa and his Chief Helper and the Blue Dragon returned to the North Pole at 11:45pm on Christmas Eve. Everyone was happy to see them back to the North Pole, and they were all clapping as Santa and the Chief Helper and the Blue Dragon walked into Santa Claus' house. "Fait accompli" (mission accomplished) said Santa Claus. Santa announced that the Christmas party can start right away, and it did start right away. At midnight, there were loud shouts of Merry Christmas! There were hugs and kisses and handshakes.

The party ended at 3am.

The merriment at the North Pole went on until January 2. The team went through their feedback and process improvement cycle every year while Prince Ademola Jnr and Princess Pauline were onboard as Santa Claus and Chief Santa Helper. They also continued the break cycle of February 15 to September 15 for Santa's crew every year. Despite increasing number of kids to deliver gifts to around the world, Santa's teams were able to finish the project each year on December 18. Santa gave the crew five days off every year before the delivery day of December 24. For the next eight years, Ted Johnson waited for Santa and the Chief Santa Helper every Christmas Eve for milk and cookies and biscuits in the Kingdom of London. After ten years of knowing Ted and his family, Santa granted

Ted his wish of coming to help at the North Pole as an intern. His internship continued for several years. Everyone in the North Pole liked Ted Johnson, and he was having the best time of his life. He continued his studies online during his time in the North Pole. He used the video-conferencing to keep in touch with his friends and family while at the North Pole.

As planned and as promised, Santa and his Chief Helper stopped over every Christmas Eve for tea and cookies with their daddy and mummy. They also spent three months of their annual six-month break from the North Pole with the King and Queen of the Kingdom of Edmonton. The King always showed kin interest in what was going on in the North Pole. He provided wise counsel to his Princess and Prince whenever they had challenges in the North Pole

63

operations and missions. The King and the Queen told Princess Pauline and Prince Ademola Jnr that they were very proud of the great work Ademola and Pauline were doing in the North Pole. Prince Ademola Jnr always wondered why the King and Queen were so interested in the North Pole Project.

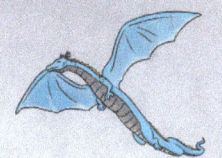

Part F

A NEW KING AND QUEEN
IN THE KINGDOM OF EDMONTON

Three days before the return of Princess Pauline and her brother Prince Ademola Jnr to the North Pole, just after breakfast, the King and Queen of the Kingdom of Edmonton summoned them to the study room within the King's chambers. The King and the Queen and Pauline and Ademola Jnr all took their usual seats in the study room in the King's chambers. The King and Queen started by thanking Princess Pauline and Prince Ademola Jnr for coming to this meeting. He used this occasion to thank them for the great work that they

were both doing in the North Pole and with the Christmas Eve project. He commended them for the effective management of the resources made available to them resulting in successful missions year after year. "I have called both of you here today, this morning to give you two important news". Said the King.

The King continued: "I would like to inform you two that the North Pole is a part of and wholly-owned by us, the Kingdom of Edmonton. It has been owned by us for three generations. The funding required every year has been provided by us through a subsidiary of one of our Royal trading companies. Our princes and princesses and princes and princesses from other kingdoms have been sent to the North Pole's Santa project. So that they acquire skills and additional wisdom that will help them to be successful

Kings and Queens in their Kingdoms. All the monies and materials used in the production of gifts for the Christmas Eve projects are provided by the Kingdom of Edmonton. The food, accommodation, running expenses and the weekly allowance and paid vacation including flights are all provided by the King and Queen of Edmonton. It has been a charitable effort to give back to the children around the world. It is a secret, and you two must keep it a secret as everyone has done in the last three generations."

Princess Pauline and Prince Ademola were surprised by this secret; their eyes and mouths were wide open. When they got their composure back, Ademola Jnr was now clear as to the reason the King was always interested in knowing what was happening in the North Pole. He was surprised how the King knew so much about

everything in the North Pole. The King was once a Santa Claus. Wow! Another surprise from the King was that more than half the population of the North Pole both men and women are part of the King's Regiment in the Army of the Kingdom of Edmonton. They are there to protect the North Pole, the Santa's Christmas Eve project and the non-military population. The King said that a lot of diamonds, gold and other precious commodities like Oil and Gas are buried underneath the North Pole that we have become envied by Kings and peoples of other Kingdoms. The King said "Santa Claus is always the administrator of the North Pole, and Santa Claus is either a young Prince or a retired General from the Kingdom's military sent there to secure the fort for us". "You and your sister have done a marvelous job" said the King and the Queen.

The King continued to the next big news. He said: "I will be stepping down from the throne next year along with your mum, the

Queen. We are both getting old, and we want to do some traveling while we are still strong. We want to visit our cousins in other kingdoms around the world. We want to visit the North Pole this year before it gets too cold". The King further said: "We will be visiting the North Pole this October from 17th to 19th. Both of you are in your prime; it will be a great time to start next year; for you to commence your reign as Queen and King. Prince Ademola and Princess Pauline wanted to know who will take over as Santa Claus and Chief Santa Helper. The King said: "Ted Johnson". Prince Ademola Jnr said he was too young and not a prince or a retired general of the Kingdom of Edmonton. The King told Prince Ademola Jnr that Ted is older than the age they were when they started going to the North Pole to volunteer. Ted has a lot of passion for the Santa Claus project in the North Pole. We have received great reports about his attitude and

work ethics since he came to the North Pole. His parents have sent his school reports to me; all his grades have shot up since he started to volunteer at the North Pole.

The assurance from the King gave Prince Ademola Jnr and Princess Pauline some peace in the King's plan. The King told Princess Pauline and Prince Ademola Jnr that the coronation will be on next June 12 – the family day in the Kingdom of Edmonton. It will be their last mission to the North Pole as Santa Claus and Santa's Chief Helper. The King wanted the two of them to be back from the North Pole by April 30 to start the process of ascension to the throne. The King said he had informed Mr. and Mrs. Johnson that Ted will be the next Santa Claus in North Pole, but they cannot be the one to break the news to Ted. It will be Prince Ademola Jnr or Santa Claus

who will break the news to Ted. "Take Ted along to your Christmas Eve mission so that Ted can get a feel of the mission and to know how the routing and timing are done with the help of NORAD and GPS". Prince Ademola Jnr and Princess Pauline will according to tradition be available to support the new Santa Claus – Ted Johnson. The King said that the last and most important part of the second news on coronation was that there will be a King and a Queen crowned. Princess Pauline looked at Prince Ademola Jnr, and he looked at her wondering what the King was talking about when he said King and Queen will be crowned. Princess Pauline asked: "Daddy! How is it possible to have a King and Queen when Ademola Jnr has not yet married?" The King said: "My dear children! Worry not! For everything is under control. The plan is based on the new royal succession standard all the progressive royal homes are

implementing around the world. The new royal succession standard states that the first-born child in line to the throne whether a male child or female child gets to become the next monarch in that Kingdom. You and your brother were born before this new royal succession standard and according to the old standard; the first male child automatically becomes the next King".

The King continued: "We chose Ademola Jnr as the next King then when he was born. But we have a new succession standard, and we believe it is fair to have a joint heir and heiress blending the new and old succession standards one final time. It makes Prince Ademola Jnr a King and Princess Pauline a Queen. Both of you will be joint rulers of the Kingdom of Edmonton effective June 12". There was excitement in the air courtesy of Princess Pauline and Prince

Ademola Jnr. They were both dancing and singing inside the King's office. The King said that he is confident that the joint rulers will do well because they have had the best training in school and hands-on in the North Pole. The King further said that the meeting was adjourned and that Princess Pauline and Prince Ademola Jnr should know that there will be no more monkeying around. It is a serious business. Princess Pauline and Prince Ademola Jnr left the King's study humming a song the King could not figure out.

The next day they all went fishing together, and it was fun as usual. They decided to return the next day for another round of fishing. It was as fun as the previous day's fishing trip. On the third day; September 14, it was time for Princess Pauline (Santa's Chief Helper) and Prince Ademola Jnr (Santa Claus) to return to the North

Pole for their last mission trip. The Blue Dragon was ready for the trip and was waiting for Pauline and her brother Ademola Jnr to emerge from the Palace doors. They came out after breakfast at 7:55am. The King and the Queen came out for final kisses and hugs. They said: "See you in October!" The Prince and Princess said good-byes and then they were gone. On this trip, they planned to stop by the borough of Chelsea in the Kingdom of London to pick up a special guest, the next Santa Claus; Ted Johnson. After three hours of flying, they arrived at Ted's house. Mr. and Mrs. Johnson insisted that they should come in for a quick tea and cookies. They said "okay we shall if you insist Mr. and Mrs. Johnson".

When they got inside, they met Ted's sisters for the first time. They were very excited to meet a Princess and Prince from the

Kingdom of Edmonton. They introduced themselves as Tasha (oldest), Philippa (second) and Melissa (third). The sisters saw the Blue Dragon for the first time. They said: "Wow! It is the Blue Dragon of Legends". The Prince and Princess and Ted's parents finished their tea and cookies. It was time to leave. Prince Ademola Jnr, Princess Pauline and Ted Johnson climbed onto the carriage on the Blue Dragon. So began the journey from the Kingdom of London to the North Pole. They took a different route based on the guidance from NORAD and arrived two hours ahead of schedule. As usual, their presence electrified the atmosphere in the North Pole. Prince Ademola mentioned that there will be an extended kick off meeting the next day before production starts for the next Christmas Eve project. Everyone went to bed early to get enough rest before production started.

After breakfast on September 15, everyone in Santa's House assembled for the project kick-off meeting in Santa's Hall. Santa Claus stood to address everyone present. He greeted everyone good morning and he welcomed everyone back from their breaks and vacation. He informed all of them about three very important announcements he wanted to make. He pleaded for their attention. He said: "The first announcement is that this will be the last mission on the North Pole for me as Santa Claus and for my sister as Santa Chief Helper. We must return to the Kingdom of Edmonton latest by April 10 on the orders of our dad and mum; the King and Queen of the Kingdom of Edmonton. We are going to be crowned as the joint King and Queen of the Kingdom of Edmonton and its territories on the 12th of June of next year". He further said: "The other

76

announcement is Ted Johnson will be replacing me as the next Santa Claus effective April 10 of next year. We ask that you give him the love and support you have shown to me and my sister during all the years we spent with you in the North Pole. He is committed, hardworking and enthusiastic which I believe are the key attributes to succeed in the North Pole and life generally".

Santa Claus continued: "Lastly, the King and Queen of the Kingdom of Edmonton will be visiting the North Pole including Santa's house from October 17 to 19. They are coming to see for themselves all the great work you are all doing here and to show their appreciation and gratitude. They will be staying in Santa's house; in the guest rooms." After these announcements, there was avery large applause for these once in a lifetime announcement.

Then Santa Claus asked the Chief Helper to ask Ted Johnson to come into the room. There was another burst of applause when Ted came in his full Santa Claus regalia as a show and tell for everyone in Santa's House to see what he looks like as Santa Claus. Santa Claus asked Ted "How is the Santa's regalia?" Ted answered "Ho Ho Ho Ho Ho." "Ted, how do you feel?" Asked Santa. Ted responded "Ho Ho Ho Ho Ho." Santa declared: "North Pole! We have a new Santa Claus in the house!" There was another round of applause in the North Pole.

Furthermore, Santa Claus mentioned that Ted Johnson will be part of the mission trip to distribute gifts to all the children of the world on December 24. Santa Claus informed the house that after the kick-off meeting today there will be no production until tomorrow. Instead there will be a special banquet and light music for

everyone for the rest of the day. True to Santa's words, after the kick-off meeting the banquet was set, and the merriment started and lasted for the rest of the day. Everyone present at the banquet got opportunities to socialize with the outgoing Santa Claus and the incoming Santa Claus and the outgoing Chief Santa Helper. They got to personally thank Prince Ademola Jnr (Santa Claus) and Princess Pauline (Santa's Chief Helper) for the great job that they did over the years since they have been coming to the North Pole. They were all very happy with the choice of the next Santa Claus – Ted Johnson. He is amiable, hardworking and ready to learn. Soon it was time to shut the banquet down so that everyone can have a great night rest before the new production start day of September 16.

After the one-day delay, the production of the gifts for the upcoming Christmas Eve distribution started. Everyone was pumped

up for the production season. They worked their routine with the Chief Santa Helper managing the project. And the outgoing Santa Claus spent time coaching and preparing the incoming Santa Claus in the various activities that were going to be his responsibilities when he took over the reign of the North Pole especially the Christmas Eve project. With everyone working so hard, the time flew by so quickly as they worked from Mondays to Fridays and from mornings until early evenings. They all enjoyed what they were doing, and it was fun work that put smiles on the faces of little children and put happiness in their hearts. Finally, the production was completed on December 17 by the highly motivated team in Santa's house. Santa asked the team to take time off to rest and enjoy themselves until the morning of December 24. It is the morning of December 24 when the crew of the Blue Dragon, the outgoing Santa,

the incoming Santa and Santa's Chief Helper will set out for the gifts distribution.

During the production cycle on October 17 to 19, the King and Queen of the Kingdom of Edmonton visited the North Pole as planned. The King and Queen visited on a low key. They met with the key staff in the North Pole and the King was able to give his appreciation for the great work the North Pole staffs were doing to protect the environment in the North Pole. He told the staff in Santa's house that the great gifts they produce put joy in the hearts of children the world over. The King and Queen spent some private time with Santa Claus and Santa's Chief Helper. They went fishing and polar bear sighting together. The King and Queen were given a royal tour of the facilities that service the North Pole and Santa's

house. The King and Queen were very impressed and satisfied with everything they saw and did in the North Pole and Santa's house. The King and Queen returned to the Kingdom of Edmonton on October 19. Before they left they gave their daughter and son a big kiss and hug and told them to stop by on Christmas Eve for tea and cookies. During the King and Queen's visit to the North Pole, they were officially introduced to Ted Johnson who was the incoming Santa Claus. They were really happy to meet Ted Johnson.

It is the D (Distribution) – Day, December 24. Everyone in Santa's house woke up early to help load up all the packages for distribution to the children of the world. After loading had been completed, Santa Claus, the Chief Santa Helper, and the incoming Santa Claus climbed onto the carriage of the Blue Dragon. Everyone in Santa's house waved goodbyes to them as they commenced their journey.

The crew returned the goodbyes and blew kisses to them and off they went. The mission was pretty routine for Santa Claus and his Chief Helper but not so for Ted Johnson (the incoming Santa). The Santas brought the GPS, and they were using the guidance of NORAD to ensure that Ted got a feel of the devices in the field. They moved from house to house and from Kingdom to Kingdom dropping off gifts for the little children of the world. While in the Kingdom of London, Santa's crew decided to stopover in Ted's house in the Borough of Chelsea to have some tea and biscuits just like the good old days. Also, to visit Ted's parents and his three sisters.

The incoming Santa (Ted) led the way into his family's house using the secret Santa access door having been shown by the

outgoing Santa how to access the secret Santa access. Ted's family was surprised to see Santa and his crew inside the house without using the front door. Their joy overshadowed their bewilderment. Even though Ted's sisters were older than him, they were all very thrilled to see him as Santa Claus. They gave big hugs to him and Santa Claus and the Chief Helper of Santa. Mr. and Mrs. Johnson also gave Santa Claus and his crew hugs. After the exchange of pleasantries, they quickly settled down for the milk and biscuits. Santa Claus gave gifts to the Johnson family with another set of hugs and kisses as they departed to continue their mission around the world. That was the last stop in the Kingdoms of Europe, and it was time to cross the great Atlantic Ocean to the Kingdoms of the Americas. They flew over the Atlantic Ocean with ease.

In the various Kingdoms in the Americas, they moved from house to house, Kingdoms to Kingdoms until they got to the King's Palace in the Kingdom of Edmonton for their usual tea and cookies with the King and Queen of the Kingdom of Edmonton. The King and Queen were very happy to see them including Ted; the incoming Santa Claus. The Palace staff set the table for them. They commenced the eating and drinking right away. They chatted about the upcoming coronation of the Prince and Princess and the progress in the North Pole and Santa's house, and they also chatted about Ted's new assignment. The King and Queen said they were delighted that Ted agreed to become the new Santa Claus and Head of the North Pole. The King assured him that Prince Ademola Jnr and his sister Princess Pauline would be there to support him anytime he had questions or concerns regarding the North Pole or Santa's house and the Christmas Eve project. Then it was time to move again to the final stop that was the Kingdom of Hawaii before heading back to the

85

North Pole. They all got hugs from the King and Queen before they left for Hawaii Kingdom.

The journey to Hawaii was quick, and the three of them split up to separately give out the gifts and as a result they were done in one hour. So, they started their journey back to the North Pole. They arrived at the North Pole at 10:50pm that was a record time. As usual, everyone in Santa's house was very jubilant and being Santa Claus' and his Chief Helper's last trip, they decided to start the Christmas party one hour earlier than the usual time. The trumpet was blown, the horn sounded and the party started. Everybody was so happy that you could feel the electricity in the air. There was a special banquet to go with the celebration. At midnight, there was a huge roar of merry Christmas with hugs and kisses and the party continued until 3am on Christmas day. Most of them skipped their breakfast and slept in until lunch time. Santa Claus had announced during the party that there would be a holiday for everyone until 3rd of January for the usual review and lessons learned meeting. The daily banquet continued until 2nd of January for all those who stayed back for the holiday season.

On 3rd of January, the production team got together to review the last production cycle and the lessons learnt. The Chief Santa Helper was assigned the task of coordinating the review meetings. Santa Claus spent his time preparing and assuring the incoming Santa (Ted) for his new role. All the reviews and training ended on February 14 to allow everyone in Santa's house to commence their six-month break that started on February 15. Prince Ademola Jnr and

Princess Pauline decided that they will travel down finally to the Kingdom of Edmonton on 1st of March to help the King and Queen in preparing for their coronation. Ted said he would leave for London at the end of March so that he could do some studies. Princess Pauline and Prince Ademola Jnr informed the King and Queen of Edmonton that they will arrive 1st of March instead of 10th of April to give a helping hand in the preparations. Santa Claus and the Chief Santa Helper informed incoming Santa Claus (Ted) that he should call them any time he had concerns or questions on any issue regarding the North Pole or Santa's house.

On 28th of February, Prince Ademola Jnr and Ted Johnson officially signed the papers that put Ted Johnson in charge of the

North Pole and Santa's house as the bona fide Santa Claus. Princess Pauline signed as the witness. Ted requested for a Dragon from Galaxyland in the Kingdom of Edmonton. The Red Dragon was delivered on 27th of February. He said: "Cool" and "Sweet" When he saw the Red Dragon. The next day 1st of March, the Blue Dragon was loaded up with Princess Pauline and Prince Ademola's properties. At the goodbye stage, Princess Pauline started to sob, and everyone including Ted and Prince Ademola Jnr joined in the crying Pauline started. The journey was delayed by 30 minutes until everyone was able to compose themselves. Hugs and kisses were given and off they went from the North Pole to the Kingdom of Edmonton. Using the secret route, they arrived Edmonton in two hours. There was a large delegation of people who waited to receive them upon arrival in Edmonton. They were clapping and singing and dancing. The

Queen and Princess Pauline started to cry. The King and Prince Ademola Jnr refused to cry.

After the welcoming ceremony for Princess Pauline and Prince Ademola Jnr, they had a brief private meeting with the King and Queen, who gave them a brief rundown of preparations to date. Some tasks were assigned to the Prince and Princess since they arrived earlier than the expected date of 10th of April. Everyone concentrated on the tasks they were assigned and by 31st of May, everything was completed. The only remaining items were set-up related. The set-up by the Palace staff was planned for two to three days before 12th of June which is the Royal Family Day in the Kingdom of Edmonton. There was a break given to everyone working on the coronation project from 31st of May until 8th of June when guests and Royals would start to arrive from all over the world for the double coronation in the Kingdom of Edmonton. It was the world's first double coronation. Everyone was eager to witness it. The set-up team commenced their work just as the guests were arriving the Kingdom of Edmonton. The Palace staff set-up was completed on 11th of June.

On 12th of June, the Royal Square was filled, and the entire Kingdom was in a party mood; celebrating the coronation of the new King and co-ruler Queen. The outgoing King and Queen briefed the Prince and Princess about the Golden Sword of the Spirit of God - the creator and protector of the Heavens and the Earth. The new King and Queen were shown how to call for the Sword and how to use it to protect themselves and the people of the Kingdom of Edmonton.

Once the ceremony of the Sword of the Spirit of God was completed, the Prince and Princess moved to the Pentecostal Chapel in the Palace where only special guests were invited into. They both rededicated their lives to God and took a vow to serve God and rule only as stated in the Bible. They assumed the role of mother and father for the people of the Kingdom of Edmonton. The Pastor of the Chapel prayed for them and asked them to cooperate with each other in the discharge of their duties. He said they should not let any man or woman come in between them and the service of their people. The pastor asked them to remain in the Spirit to maintain the divine wisdom God has bestowed upon each of them.

After the Chapel ceremony, it was time for the open crowning ceremony in the Royal Square. They all proceeded to the Square,

which was right in front of the Palace. The two boxes where the King's and Queen's Crowns were housed were laid on their stand. The Square was filled with representatives of the royal families from other Kingdoms around the world. It also contained different segments of the Edmonton populace. Ted Johnson (Santa Claus) and his family were there, and everyone in Santa's house in the North Pole was there and ready to party and partying they did. At exactly 11:55am on 12th of June, the outgoing King and Queen of the Kingdom of Edmonton stood up from their chairs and went to the two boxes that were opened by the Palace guards. Prince Ademola Jnr and Princess Pauline went on their knees on the knee pads in front of their chairs. The King removed his crown and grabbed the King's crown from the box in front of the Prince and the Queen removed her crown and grabbed the Queen's crown from the box.

Both of them proceeded to where the Prince and Princess knelt down. The King and Queen raised the crowns toward Heaven, and they were holding it with their eyes closed to pray for the crowns and the new wearers of the crown.

At exactly 12 noon on 12th of June, the trumpets sounded and the King and Queen ended their prayers. The Queen placed the crown on Princess Pauline's head; first to become Queen as the first child. And the King placed the crown in his hands on Prince Ademola's head to become King as the first male child. The crowns removed from the outgoing King and Queen were placed in the boxes and taken away never to be worn again. The trumpets sounded again to herald in a new King Ademola II and Queen Pauline I. There was a very loud and hilarious ovation for the new King and

Queen. The coronation celebrations lasted for seven days until the 18th of June before everyone departed for their cities, states and Kingdoms. The new King and Queen asked their daddy and mummy to remain in the royal guest suites inside the palace. They told Ted Johnson again to stop by every Christmas Eve during his missions around the world to give gifts and presents to the children of the world.

ABOUT THE AUTHOR

Ademola Usuanlele, B.Eng., CQA, PMP and Member of PMI; Senior Member of ASQ and AIChE

Ademola is the co-Junior Chairman/CEO of Groupe Haus Incorporated, which is headquartered in Edmonton, Alberta and has subsidiaries in two African Countries.

Ademola is a highly experienced Chemical Engineer with over 20 years of professional experience spanning oil and gas, telecoms, consulting and pharmaceuticals. He started his career as a Contract Field Engineer with Schlumberger in Nigeria and later joined Sowsco Well Services Nigeria as a Contract Field Engineer. He worked for Raylo Chemicals Inc. (now a Gilead Sciences Company) a major CMO in the biotech and pharmaceutical industry. After that he joined Biomira Inc., a leader in Cancer Vaccine Research in Edmonton, Alberta Canada as a Quality Assurance Specialist.

These days Ademola spends his time as a Consultant and a Business Generalist developing strategic and sustainable solutions for clients around the world. Ademola is an experienced Project Management Professional, PMP and an ASQ Certified Quality Auditor.

He enjoys traveling, working on complex projects, music, reading, and mentoring and learning new languages. He also enjoys spending time with his wife Christiana "Titilayo", daughter Pauline, son Ademola Jnr and his extended family. He is a past board director of Oliver Centre in Edmonton, Alberta. He is the former board national treasurer and member of Canadian Family Advisory Network (CFAN). He is the council former co-chair for the Edmonton, Alberta Canada Stollery Children's Hospital's Family-Centred Care Council (FCCC). He is a former section Audit Chair and former
Member Chair of Edmonton Section of American Society for Quality (ASQ). He is the founder and board President of Ademola Usuanlele Charitable Foundation. Ademola Usuanlele is a former board director of both Canadian Council for Africa (CCAfrica) and Canada-Nigeria Chamber of Commerce.

www.ingramcontent.com/pod-product-compliance
Lightning Source LLC
Chambersburg PA
CBHW080825020726
47501CB00009B/2430